Poetry by James Humphrey

Mize & Kathy
(1998) VOLUME

LĒF
(1997) VOLUME

SIZ
(1997) VOLUME

BUD
(1996) VOLUME

ICE
(1989) CHAPBOOK

The Athlete
(1988) VOLUME

*After I'm Dead,
Will My Life Begin?*
(1986) VOLUME

In Tribute To Survivors
(1984) CHAPBOOK

In New York City Air
(1984) CHAPBOOK

The 5¢ Poem
(1981) CHAPBOOK

The Re-Learning
(1976) VOLUME

*An Homage: The End of
Some More Land*
(1972) CHAPBOOK

The Visitor
(1972) CHAPBOOK

Argument For Love
(1970) VOLUME

Mize & Kathy

James Humphrey

Poets Alive! Press   1998   New York

Copyright © 1998 by James Humphrey

All rights reserved. Except for brief passages quoted in a newspaper, magazine, radio, or television review, no part of this book may be reproduced in any form or by any means, electronic or mechanical, including photocopying and recording, or by any information storage and retrieval system, without permission in writing from the publisher.

Manufactured in the United States of America
Poets Alive! Press on acid-free paper.

Some of *Mize & Kathy* first appeared in *SIZ*, (PA!P, 1997), changed somewhat for this book. The editors wish to thank James Humphrey for agreeing to make minor changes for this collection.

Statement page, "Reflections of My Life" sung by THE MARMALADE.
Reprinted by permission Rhino Records.

Bernard Malamud statement reprinted with permission from the Bernard Malamud estate.

Cover art: *Orchid*, book design & photography: Saroyan Humphrey

Special limited edition of 500 books.
26 signed/designed "First day of publication"
by James and Saroyan Humphrey

Library of Congress Cataloging in Publication Data

Humphrey, James, 1939-
    Mize & Kathy / James Humphrey
    I. Title
ISBN 0-936641-25-8
Acid-free paper

Poets Alive! Press
81 Spruce Street
Yonkers, NY
10701

SPECIAL LIMITED EDITION 500 BOOKS

"*The grievings of people in trouble,*

reflections of my life.

Oh, how they fill my eyes.

All my sorrows, sad tomorrows."

THE MARMALADE

Dedicated to all sexually abused and neglected children, teens, and adults with deep compassion, love, and strength to fight back.

It is my conviction that dignity and wisdom often are achieved only through trials from which we cannot escape.

BERNARD MALAMUD

1914-1986

Contents

13 / Winter

23 / Spring

43 / Summer

71 / Fall

77 / Winter

First day of publication, March 1, 1998,
26 signed/designed by James and Saroyan Humphrey.

Mize & Kathy

Winter

ONE

When a boy, Mize's favorite
steep
swirling
whirling
forever
twisting
curving
natural mind-blowing
sled racing hill, he now at late 19
crouched in racing start at its
summit,
pumping up with deep breaths
set to challenge it this
Empty
night
of
the
day
his
dad's
body was buried.

winter

Ice crusted, hard deep snow
under a billion aluminum stars,
skinny sickle moon,
feeling he's in a giant snow globe,
yells at the Heavens,
"THIS LAST RUN'S FOR YOU, DAD!"

Body slams prone against racer
his dad built him when 10,
its waxed steel runners
dance over iced snow.
The ballet begins,
snow globe shaking. . .

TWO

His dad collapsed packing hen eggs.
No warning. Heart just quit.
He was 61.
The egg man found him the next morning.

Mize and hired hands pickaxed
through ice
down
into

frozen
ground
making
Whil's final earthly bed.

Startled eyes and sadness from the
nearby woods was felt by Mize and
one of the hands, sharing their
mutual feelings momentarily
looking at each other — *All* of it
in their eyes beyond the limits of
words.
Even the few remaining visible
withered leaves seemed in
mourning.

Mize was Whil's only child. He,
Kathy, his steady since they'd
drag raced a few days before the
Zephyr High School Prom, the young
parish priest, friends, neighbors,
buried Whil next to his wife JoAnn
on his 2,000 acre spread. She had
painlessly died from cancer in
2 weeks at 35. Mize was 7.

winter

THREE

Mize stood next to the elevated
waist-high unlined pine coffin,
right hand often holding
his dad's folded hands
as he spoke to the small gathering.

"Dad was my best friend.

"I was his.

"We told each other many times,
nearly always making eye contact.
Hugs and spoken 'I love you,'
were common in our language.

"Growing up, dad and I and a few
hands, worked our you-know-whats
off building the farm into what it
is today. Sometimes when an
unfamiliar car or pickup drove by,
I'd wonder if he was an inspiration
to anyone in the vehicle — just the
way he moved was a strong, confident

statement from his deeper self — so
I asked him if he ever gave a
thought to it."

"Naw," he laughed, "They'd more
likely be thinking how important
they are, and I should look up to
them."

"Another time I said he reminded me
of Henry David Thoreau because he
kept a journal and made entries
at least once a day. He came right
back with, 'Einstein thought of
himself as a farmer.'

"The earth was dad's teacher — that
and his heart. If he'd lived 30
more years — or longer — senility
would never enter him, and I can't
imagine him a wrinkled stalk.

"In my heart, dad will always be
a young shoot — he walked his own
road, and he kept that road clear.

winter

He was a great risk taker and the
champ of determination. He was a
wizard at squeezing nickels where
they were supposed to be squeezed,
but he wasn't cheap or stingy. All
of us here know how big and generous his heart was.

"He told me he listened to Sunday
baseball double-headers right up
to the end of the '50s, then began
slacking off. Said it quit being
a game played from the heart — from
every pore of the body with
strength and courage the players
didn't think they had — that it
became a 'Money show.'

"Dad had a lot of ball heroes — the
most common names we all know — he
talked most about Hank Saur, George
Kell, and Al Dark. But there was a
16 year old who played center field
for the Cardinal organization just
that one season — then vanished. To

this day Humphrey is the youngest
guy to wear a major league uniform.
It bothered dad that he couldn't find out
what happened to him.

"When I graduated high school,
I renewed my promise to dad
to keep the farm batting a solid 400,
if anything would happen to him.
Two entries from his journal
I'd like to close with:

'My opinion doesn't matter, the
world does as it pleases. . .

'In order to gain,
we have to lose. . .'"

FOUR

On Whil's memorial stone
was inscribed one of his
most repeated beliefs,

"The Joy of Effort"

ONE

Changing classes a few days before
Zephyr's high school graduation,
Mize
walks
w/
senior
buddies
a
cool
senior's
distance
behind
a
sharp senior girl.

Being the leader, Mize nonchalantly
mumbles,
"Where'd the looker w/ headlights
all her own,
pointin' straight-out way-up high
appear from — a new transfer?"
Sergio, his right hand answers,
"Where yuh bin, Man — 'Skinny K's'

spring

bin in our class since
kindergarten
— just filled out this year
— nice fanny too, huh?"

"What a holiday she'd be!"

"Aw, Man — forget her — just another
nothin' honor roll virgin, leaving for
college soon as the all-night
senior dance/breakfast ends
and she ain't takin' a bus!"

"She got a date?"

"C'mon, Mize, get it in gear
— who'd date her?
The wimp biology and science worms
are staying home with mommy —
c'mon!"

TWO

Next Friday at the A&W,
parked alone in his spotless Olds 442,

MIZE & KATHY

Mize sees 'Skinny K' in his rear-view
mirror slowly tooling by in a
chopped & channeled, rolled &
tucked leather-appointed,
hand-rubbed cherry '56 2-door Ford
Crown Vic!
Several girls were with her. She
purposely parks two cars down from
Mize, the sparkling chrome bumper
over the lip of the car-hop's
sidewalk.

He pretends not to know she's there.
Kathy knows what he's doing.
She ignores him.
The girls order.

Mize sips a Coke.

While they're eating burgers &
fries, he strolls over to Kathy's
door, smiles in at her over the
window food tray, and coolly braces
his hand against the fender top.

s p r i n g

In a friendly voice, she orders,
"Please don't touch the paint."
　Surprised, Mize straightens up.
"Well — excuse me!"

"You don't let anyone touch
　your car."

"Got me there — engine as hot as the
　rest of her looks?"

"Just like a giving person gives everything
　she has in her."

"WHOA! I'm outta your league!"

"Come on, Big man on campus
　— give me a try."

"One of us will fall short
　— can't give what we don't have."

"WHOA! Listen to you—what do you
　say — loser pays for food and drinks
　— the drag strip, OK?"

"It's closed at night."

"So's the swimming pool
  — that doesn't stop you and
  Heather."

"We broke up."

"How come?"

"I was told you were bashful and
  dull."

"Guess it depends on whose
  company I'm in. . ."

"What's-her-name joined the herd
  — thinks acting mature is being
  unfeeling — like too many parents
  I know."

"Well, Mister 442, we gonna gab
  the night away, or race?"

"Crank it up."

spring

THREE

At the strip, the girls scramble out.
One stands several feet in front of
the white, painted starting line,
between the two revving beauties.
Flashlight in right hand, left at
her side,
palm open,
calmly
pushes
it
down
—*Suddenly* waves the flash,
leaping high into the headlight
splayed night!

Rear tires smoke biting the
asphalt.
Side-by-each, 4-speed short Hurst
floor shifts slam into second!
Mize is impressed: Kathy's bumper
just inches ahead of his!
She hits third,
jumps a bit further into lead!

Mize misses a speed shift,
recovers
but loses.

Kathy and Mize avoid eye contact.
Both turn their hot machines around,
head back to the starting line.
He keeps driving.
Kathy stops. Her cheering friends
climb in.
On the highway — In the distance,
Kathy sees the Olds 442's taillights,
She wonders what Mize is thinking.

It was his first loss.

At the root beer stand,
he pays the tab,
giving the car-hop a generous tip,
 walks over to Kathy's window.

"You're really something — what's
 your name?"

"Kathy — you just missed third

s p r i n g

— could've happened to anyone."

"Listen, if you don't mind riding in
a second-place car, how about
going to the senior dance and breakfast?"

"You've got it, Champ!"

The All-Night Senior Dance/Breakfast

ONE

Mize nervously knocks at Kathy's
grandparent's front door
wearing a smart rented tux, feeling
overdressed.

An angel in strapless white formal
emerges!

He opens the car door for her saying,
"My God! You are Beautiful!"

"So are you," she returns looking
up at him.
Opening his door,
Mize takes a deep breath,
says inside himself,
"You're doing pretty good for a
 coward,"

spring

slides in and fires the engine.

Kathy asks, "Going to pin my
corsage on?"

Erotic reds and oranges blaze in
him!
Takes the orchid from the box,
suddenly realizing there's no place
to pin it!

Kathy comes to the rescue,
"Glad I'm not you."
She touches where she wants it
pinned.

With the aid of the gods,
he somehow accomplishes this
without brushing her breast.
"I don't get it — I've been out with
plenty of girls — but now I'm so
goddamn nervous!"

TWO

In the festive decorated gym,
Mize and Kathy danced with each other,
not in spite of each other,
which is common today.
Yet he was still tight inside.
During the fourth slow dance
Kathy whispered,
"Mize you're ruining your image
 — loosen up and hold me tight. . . "
Brilliant turquoise, hot pinks,
deep raspberry, watermelon red and
wisteria, exploded in him.
He
did.

THREE

About 4 A.M., after the buffet
breakfast, while Mize was driving
back to her grandparents,
she said,
"I've never been to the gravel pit
 — let's go for a swim!"

s p r i n g

"Aw, it will be packed."

"That'll be safe for you. . . "

   He parked in front of the house and
said "OK."
Kathy lifted her formal and silk slip
halfway up her perfect thighs, ran
into the house, quickly leaving it
— still running happily — swinging
a lavender string bikini.
Mize was going Krazy inside;
outwardly he stayed cool.
She hopped in, fresh Chantilly
perfume mixed with a little sweat and
her natural sexually aroused body
perfume, tore through the guy just as
it was all supposed to do, and as he
had trained himself all through
high school forced himself to play the
cool role.

"My suit's in the trunk."

"Oh," Kathy teased, "didn't think you

wore one after dark."

FOUR

Narrow cow path beneath big, old oaks,
only passage to the hidden gravel pit.
In the moon's full light, Kathy tells
Mize the names of the flowers, plants, and
herbs:
"Daisies, Buttercups, Rhododendron,
Shinleaf, Cow Parsnip, Sweet Cicely."

"Well — I came to swim — biology is
behind me."
He dashes for the small beach,
is surprised no one else is there.
Strips,
puts on his tight suit and dives into
icy dark emerald water,
scaring Spoonbill mates into flight.

From the path, Kathy had seen Mize
peel. Surging raw adrenal
excited her in ways she'd never felt.
She raced to where his tux laid,

spring

feeling great happiness.
She yells out at him,
"I'll strip for you if you've got a
recording of Billy Rose's 'Stripper!'"

"That's big talk for a virgin!"

"Watch!"

He does.

She does.

Continuing to face him, she puts on
her string bikini then yells,
"COME TO SHORE — I HAVE TO TELL YOU
SOMETHING IMPORTANT!"

Mize moans and thinks while
side-stroking to shore, "It's *BIG*
surprise time, farm boy
— her seventh-grade science teacher
got her first."

FIVE

"I don't have parents."

"That's why you live with who you do?"

"When I was in sixth grade, it was
just another ordinary day walking
into the house after school.
. . . except the horror-of-horrors
happened! On the kitchen table was a
short letter in daddy's writing that
read, *'You were a misake*
— someone else's
— we're moving on
— go live wih your
adopted grandparents
— they're expecting you.'

"It wasn't signed. Not even initialed.
They took *everything* — even all the
towels and linens."

They sat down on Mize's tux jacket.
She laid her cheek softly against

spring

his heart.
He held her close that way and asked,
"Do you have any idea why they'd do
such an awful thing?"

"Because I wouldn't fuck him!"

"You serious?"

"Mize, you're the first person
I've told — not even at confession."

"How did you stop him?"

"First with a ball bat
 — then mace — I had it with me
everywhere — and I mean *everywhere!*"

"Did you tell the school principal
or the police?"

"I just told you, Dumb-Dumb — you're
the first to know."

"Why didn't you tell someone who

could help?"

"Guys are so stupid! Think there's
a logical answer for everything!
I know a girl who did tell the police
what her uncle was doing to her.
Guess what the brilliant chief did?"

"I'm getting the picture — he went and
talked it over with the uncle — right?"

"You got it!"

"And 'good ol' unc' really made the
girl wish she'd kept her mouth
shut. . ."

"It was just a little bit worse
— she killed herself. . ."

"I really want to say something
comforting, but all I can think of
is, 'Oh shit !'"

"The female I believed was my mother,

spring

made it with other guys — I walked in
on her at least 4 times when I was
5 — who knows how many times since.
At first I just thought that was how
it was with every man and woman."

"As you got older you started
putting it together."

"Maybe I put it together too good."

"Whada you mean?"

"What if I'm like my mother. . ."

Mize didn't know what to say.
He sensed that whatever came out
would be inadequate, so he kept
his mouth shut, hugged Kathy
tighter.

They watched the magnificent
sun come up, then he drove her
to her grandparent's house.

Summer

Off to the University

ONE

Mize and Kathy's gramp put her wardrobes over the new, large white suitcases in the Vic's backseat. "That's it," Gramp Conlee says, "The 6-hour drive to Iowa City will get you there about suppertime — say, Mize, has Kathy mentioned our farm is for sale?"

"Nope."

"You and your dad have built yours into quite a spread — maybe you've had enough, and are making 'city plans,' like so many fellas are."

"No — I'm stayin' here."

"Ever consider buyin' your own place?"

summer

"I promised dad I'd keep our place."

TWO

A couple hours out, Mize turns his
Olds into a truck stop for fuel
and food. Kathy follows.

In a booth eating hot fries and
spooning thick malts Mize asks,
"How do you feel now about what you
told me last night?"

"Uneasy — awkward — Oh I don't know
— confused, I guess."

"About what?"

"How do I know I can trust you?"

"Well, then, there, now. You shared
the worst experience of your life
with me and no one else. That
should tell you something."
"What will you think of me

next week — or the week after that?"

"Danger lurks in the summer moon."

"I'm not into 'summer love,' Mize.
Everybody likes you when you're
somebody else."

"I'm not either, but I hear it's
better than tossing pennies at what
that ol' moon does to you.

"I want you to be my girl, Kathy."

"Hmmm, we're driving to the
university so I can begin the first
day of summer session — me thinks
it's a little soon to marry."

They laugh and Kathy says,
"I suppose you grocery shop for
bachelor things — like Mrs. Paul's
frozen toast."

"Yeah—I nuke'm, but I have to move

summer

every month because the sink fills
up with greasy butter knives."

"Mize, I've had a crush on you
since early grade school, but knew
you'd never give me a second look
because I was a bean pole."

"Now you'd look great in a double-
padded snowmobile suit, thick
gloves and a welder's helmet
— Hey — changing classes before we
raced, were you purposely walking
in front of me?"

" — And that wasn't the *first* time!
God! You were blind!
Finally seeing the attraction
sparked a chemical reaction!"

"Welcome to my kingdom."

"Don't overwind your toys,
 Farm boy. . . "

"Kathy, can I ask you a question that
 just might upset you?"

"Ouch! OK."

"Do you know who your blood parents
 are?"

"To be dumped twice the first
 eleven years of my life — they just
 weren't worth knowing about.
 Mize. . . I sense your concern is
 genuine — that's not Zephyr High's
 Mister Cool — what's going on?"

"Just how I survived school. Dad's
 my teacher. The earth is his.
 Besides — after last night — well
 — maybe I grew up some."

THREE

About three years earlier, gramp
Conlee had leased a small well-kept
ordinary-size farm house outside

summer

Iowa City for Kathy.

The instant Kathy now flung open
the front door and stepped into
the lovely femininely furnished
living room, her worst fear
arrived.
It ripped out of her unconcious,
tore through her heart
— *HORRIFIED SCREAMS*
falling unheard in a distant field;
"YOU'LL ABANDON ME JUST LIKE THEY
DID — I'M ALL ALONE HERE!"

"I'm with you."

"YOU DIDN'T HEAR A GODDAMN WORD
I SAID!"

"No matter how long it takes,
I'll stay with you until
you get settled in."

"Then you'll leave and I'll never
see you again!"

"Now that's bullshit and you know it."

"Oh Mize, I'm sorry — I'm alone for
the first time in my life and I'm
scared. I hate being away from
Grampa and Gramma! I hate being
away from my bedroom! I miss my
girlfriends! I miss Zephyr!
It was familiar! I felt safe there!"

"Now you've got an A-F-G-O."

"WHAT!?"

"Another fucking growth opportunity."

"Real clever — real good timing
 — thanks!"

"I'm sorry — it was supposed to be funny
 — I should go into the
toilet with it.

"Try to see me — the person.
I'm not either of your

summer

   asshole fathers
    — I wasn't in your life
   when they were!
"Kathy, you've got an edge over them
    — you gotta grab it
    — *right now*
    — their hearts are black
    — neither has a conscience.
You live from your heart
—it's like a self-healing,
pink petalled waterlilly."

"Maybe I don't deserve to be loved."

"That's them talking — not you
  — that's what they want you to
believe."

"What if they're right. . . "

"Skinny K! You had me convinced
you overcame your abuse and became
a winner."

"What if I'm not. . . " .

Mize kicks a hole in a large
cardboard box, yanks open the front
door, leaves.
Kathy streaks after him.
Before he reaches the porch steps,
turns and looks at him
not knowing what to say or do.

He waits.

"Kathy, listen to me. I won't quit
on you. C'mon, we're just starting.
Let's give each other a chance
— maybe we'll share a big slice of
heaven. Maybe we won't — maybe we'll
get as far as a couple double orders
of fries, and that will be it
— but let's take a chance and
trust each other."

FOUR

(for Norma)

The rest of the night,

summer

Mize and Kathy fully dressed
except for sneaks, laid on the couch
only necking, French kissing, and
massaging each other's back

until the harmless soft sound of
the morning newspaper thumped on
the porch.
They sleepily smiled at each other
Kathy felt safe, protected.
Mize sensed a natural emotional
growth had taken place inside
himself, distancing him further
from the herd.

He hoped Kathy felt something
similar, but knew better than to ask.

Chicago Weekend

ONE

During mid-June Kathy met Jane. By coincidence they had two classes together. Jane introduced herself after the third one.

"Hi. I'm Jane from Chicago."

"I'm Kathy from 'Nowheresville, Iowa.' Auditing or taking it for the semester?"

"I'm definitely not auditing, but don't know if I'll be around all semester. God! I'm so far behind, I'm probably the oldest frosh here. Got time for coffee?"

"Sounds good."

During the next month Kathy and

summer

Jane hung a lot. Friendship began.
A tornado had destroyed a large
corncrib and heavily damaged the
grain elevator on Mize and his
dad's spread. This kept him away.
Spending time with Jane blocked-
out thinking about being alone.
Most importantly, it stopped her
from dwelling on the fear that
Mize would desert her.

During a humid evening while
drinking margaritas in Jane's
Iowa City apartment, she confided,
"I'm drunk enough to tell you
my most intimate secret."

"Sure you want to?"

"I read people well — I know you'd
keep it to yourself."

"But only tell me if you really
want to."

"I *really*, *really* want to!

"My parents ignored me
  — I felt invisible
  — tried making friends with
  grade school classmates
  — what do you suppose
  they called me?"

"I'll guess if you guess at what
  I was called."

"You too, K?"

"I'll bet we're running in the same
  direction. Hmmm — How 'bout
  'Puddin' Brain Jane?'"

"Wrongwrongwrongwrong!"

"Brain Jane, then."

"Now yur really off!"

"OK — Lame Jane."

summer

"Naw — *'Plain Jane'* — that's what I
was and they made me eat it until
I was a sophomore — then my tits
really bloooooomed!"

"What kinda' flowers were they?"

Both laugh and Jane says, "Next
summer my plain face started
getting really pretty — that's when
the boys began howling and tried
to eatum!"

More laughter and margaritas.

"Did you let them — or is that a bad
question?"

"Just the best jocks — and we didn't
stop with the blouse off. . ."

"Does it bother you anymore — I mean
what they called you?"

"I outgrew it — with a little help

from my fav jocks."

"Not even a little — like when
 you're lonely. . ."

"There's no time for lonely in my
 life — what'd they call you —
Curvy Kathy?"

"Don't I wish — Skinny K! That's
 what I was scarred with!"

"You'll get over it. You're away
 from all of 'em now. Being here is
 the next step of your life. The
 past will take care of itself."

"I'm not so sure about that."

"Hey, Kath! I'm going home this
 weekend — flying out from CR
 Thursday — These humid Iowa summers
 — I need a break — like to come
 and hang out at the AC'd private
 plush club with me?"

summer

"Chicago?"

"Yeah — unless my parents have moved since we met."

"Sure. Why not — Mize is still rebuilding from the tornado — Hay baling is about ready to begin — there's nothing keeping me here — Oh — I know I can't avoid your parents when we're at your home — but at the club, could we? I'm not into mothers and fathers."

"Kath, after what you went through, I wouldn't be either. Mine don't belong to the club. They're *always* vacationing somewhere. They won't be there this weekend, that's why I'm flying in."

Kathy packed a few things. Ready to leave, she picked up the phone to call Mize's farm about her plans, but the most logical rationalization

why the call wasn't necessary
entered her: *"He'll be so busy 15
hours a day he won't know it's the
weekend."*

She left believing that

THREE

Kathy was knocked for a loop inside
when a private limo met she and
Jane at O' Hare. Outwardly she took
it in stride, but when they drove
down a seemingly endless shaded
drive, and stopped at the marble
stairway to a mansion, Kathy
couldn't contain herself when she
unconsciously blurted out, "I know
a woman's best birth control is to
never shave anywhere — let me
tell you 'Plain Jane,' I'd quit
shaving permanently to live here!"

"When you told me you'd never been
out of Iowa, I wanted to give you

summer

a little surprise."

"You sure in the hell did just that,
Girl! I'm exhausted!"

"Then we'll rest tonight, and I'll
give you the dollar tour of Chicago
tomorrow — then I've got a
Fantastic thrill for you."

FOUR

The *fantastic* thrill was the air
conditioned private club
— only it wasn't a country club as
she had imagined.
It wasn't a club for families at all!

It was a swanky private strip club!

Jane introduced her to the owner.
"A fresh body for the weekend?" he
asked Jane.

"Whada you say, beautiful — wanna

give it a try — it's f-u-n."

Stunned, Kathy stammers out, "You mean you've taken your clothes off in front of all those howling barbarians?"

"Oh sure — since high school — gives me a real high."

"You don't let them put money in your garter like they're doing to that girl now, do you — please don't tell me you do."

"I do. Sometimes I go with a real rich dude for the night — that's where the money is."

"What for — surely you don't need it!"
"Like I said — it's f-u-n."

"That's just what it is little lady," the owner said. "All you have to do is give the goons a

summer

little seductive charm and style
so each of 'em thinks you're giving it
just to him — with your dynamite bod,
you're a winner — a natural — you'll
havum eating out of your tender
hand in the first 30 seconds — C'mon,
whada you say — just do it once
— nobody knows you here — then
someday you can tell your
grandchildren what their naughty
gramma did just once."

When 6, Kathy would stand on her
mother's vanity bench,
sadly look into powder-dusty
large, oval mirror, plead,
"Will someone please love me?"

When ache in
heart
so
BIG
couldn't stand it,
whisper
to

self
"I will. . . "

In tiny unsure manner almost
cry,
"how much. . . ?"

Spreading arms
wide as they'd go
sing in Big Happy voice,
"MORE THAN THE WHOLE WORLD!"

FIVE

Standing behind the bar stage curtain
in glittering silver gown, long
black gloves, Jane said,
"Baby, that's more than ordinary
stripping material — what you're
wearing is a double feature of
Mae West dialogue!"

Suddenly Jane's voice couldn't be
heard, nor the cat calls, howling
and applause from out front.

summer

Kathy couldn't hear anything. It
was a special moment, never before
experienced.

She was euphoric with *POWER!*

So sure of this feeling
she was almost serene,
standing less than 10 feet from
the flashing, waving erotic-colored
spots of splayed stars.

So sure this feeling
was within her to turn every
star sparkle into a wishing-well
brimming with bullets that would
bring *every* father at the bar
who would paw at her
to their collective knees,
begging for mercy,
and she not giving it to them.

Her permanent torment for which
she wasn't responsible, would be
worsened by entering the ecstacy

of the first spotlight.

All the barbaric noise returned.

Kathy walked to a dressing room,
changed into shorts, blouse and sneaks.

During the serene moment of power,
everything that had confused and
scared her
vanished.
She knew what she had been
driven to: a revenging snake
wrapped in such a tight coil
each strike would be fatal.

During that special moment,
she had remembered the Iowa farm boy
who probably loved her, but she
knew it would be years before she
could feel his kisses. . . if ever. . .
She knew her life had no life.
She knew it had been taken at birth.

Racing from the club into the darkness,

summer

she heard Jane call in hard voice,
"IF YOU DON'T WANTUM — I'M STAYIN'!"

SIX

On the 'red eye' flight back to
Iowa City, exhausted Kathy's
endless tape recording began,

"The beds of my life
are destined to be
littered
with nameless, faceless males

"The sight of myself will
dissolve
as will my dream to have
lemon-yellow sheets and pillow cases.

"Honest intimacy has always been
my enemy.
My body
will never be a
moist rose

*"I'm nothing but a plaything
on a leash."*

MIZE & KATHY

ONE

Making the season's only visit to the gravel pit, Kathy hadn't yet told Mize about the Chicago strip club, nor did she name the gentle marigolds, showy chrysanthemums, and striking compass plant as they climbed the narrow cow path.

"Hey, Kathy, aren't you forgetting something?"

"You tell me."

"You're not naming the flowers."

"Well, I don't feel up to it."

"Shoot — I even know the name of that one — it's a mum."

"It's a chrysanthemum."

"OK, Grumpy, whatever you say.

f a l l

I just know when ît was homecoming,
everyone calledum mums."

At water's edge, she stoops,
brushes her hand through the water.
"Brrrrrrr! Too cold for me."

"That's a bummer — last time we were
here, you stripped w/out Billy
Rose's orchestra. Me thinks there's
something buggin' you. . . "

"The water's just too cold."

"You're not lettin' college change
you into a so-called 'regular adult,'
are you?"

"That's really good — ît oughta be
framed!"

"Kathy, you seein' someone else?"

"Oh, Mize, no!"

"I know something's knawing at you
— let's talk."

"I don't know if there is, but if
I find out, I'll tell you — now,
Plow boy, make love to me like
you never have!"

TWO

Walking down the path to Mize's
442, abruptly a crazed cougar
— steel jawed trap dug into a
hind ankle, charges from the Oaks!
Mize grabs Kathy's hand yelling,
"Don't look back!" He had heard the
weak snarl and saw the dragging
trap. "WE'VE GOT A CHANCE — JUST
DON'T LOOK BACK — DON'T FALL!"

Kathy barrels into the car's driver
side, releases the trunk knob.
It pops open.
Mize yanks out his leather-cased
12-gauge automatic, still not

f a l l

looking at the cougar.

He cleanly, smoothly clears the
weapon, unsnaps the safety,
turns,
and with disciplined eyes focuses
between the animals eyes
only a few feet from leaping at his
throat!

BAMMMMM! BAMMMMM!

It's dead, jerking body rolls
against Mize's trembling legs.

Kathy jumps out yelling,
"Mize! Mize! Are you hurt!"

He screams into the
unconcerned
sky
"WHY DOES IT HAVE TO BE THIS WAY!"

Perfect Acoustics

Mize has just buried his dad.

Standing center thick bluish lake

Not breathing

All senses lifted

Stillness never experienced

Forthbursting from motionless woods

Passionate singing White-Throated Warbler

No pitch pipe, triangle, metronome, treble-clef, ligature

Nature's perfection unto itself

winter

ONE

Kathy intently watches Mize from the den window. When he gets to land, she throws on her parka, rushes outside, meeting him near her car.

He happens to catch a glimpse of her white suitcase and wardrobe in the Vic's backseat. "Tell me you're joking — You're not leaving right now, are you?"

"I'm going."

"C'mon — what are you doing? Why so sudden?"

"To me it's not sudden."

"What's going on — let's talk about whatever it is."

"I just have to leave."

"But right now? That's a little
unfair to me, don't you think?"

"I'm sorry, Mize, maybe I'm not the
person you think I am."

"You trying to say something about
not being at your house a
particular weekend last summer?"

"Oh shit — you weren't supposed
to know!"

"Know what?"

"I doubt if I'll ever talk about it
— how'd you find out I wasn't at
the house?"

"Tried to call you a couple dozen
times. I was worried about you,
Kathy, so I just drove on in.
Waited until Sunday night
— been hoping all along you'd
bring it up. . . "

winter

"That's why it was so long before
I saw you — and I called you to see
if something was wrong."

"There you go — that's how love
works."

"Mize, I don't know if I'm capable
of loving *anyone* — I'm the doll
that came with no self-esteem
— happiness can't even be an
illusion."

"What the hell happened?!"

"I just need to be alone to sort
out a lot of stuff. When I was
Skinny K, I buried myself in
school work and tutoring. Maybe
that's what I need to do now."

"Aw c'mon, we can work this out
together. Hell, we're all flawed.
There are no exceptions. Please,
Kathy, give yourself a couple more

days here. We'll just do simple
things — ice fishing, skating,
hiking, cooking, making endless
love. . . Whatever you want to do
— and we'll talk only if you
decide to — Deal?"

"I can't, Mize — really, I can't."

She walks around the car to the
driver's door, opens it. They look
at each other over the roof.

"Hang onto a dream, Skinny K. . . "

She gets in, fires up the cold engine,
lets it warm.

Mize goes into the house.
In an eternal minute, he hears
the powerful Crown Vic pull out.

He begins sobbing; leaves for his
dad's graveside. Head bowed, his
sobs become deeper, louder.

winter

Startled ring-necked pheasant mates
panic into flight

Brief dusk
Pale
Cold
Frightening

Night without light for Mize

Night without light for Kathy

Through it

Through it

I KNOW I LEARNED more about my deeper self and the human psyche writing *Mize & Kathy* that I am consciously aware. While writing this free-form improvisation, I wrote two insights I had not previously thought of quite like this, knowing that if I didn't write them, I surely wouldn't remember them. *"Experience is meaningless unless we learn from it." "Virtue is giving beyond what you think you are capable."* Mize re-taught me a special patience and tolerance so many, many years of constant deep pain and suffering was knawing away. Kathy taught me not to be judgmental, no matter how legitimate it seemed to be at the moment.

James Humphrey is an honors graduate, Brown University, 1977. He was born in Sioux City, Iowa, 1939. He counsels homeless children, orphans, abused kids, teens and adult victims of child abuse in Manhattan.

His wife of 32 years, Norma Van Vooren-Humphrey, whose father Charles Van Vooren, 1902-1956, Humphrey dedicated *BUD*, Poets Alive! Press, 1996, is a New York reference librarian. Their only child, Saroyan, named after William Saroyan, lives in San Francisco where he is a freelance art director and graphic designer.

Printed February 1998 for Poets Alive! Press by VIP Lithography, San Francisco. Designed and typeset entirely in Emigré Mrs. Eaves